FOXING DAY

Deadlights Cove, A Holiday Novella

B. PERKINS

AIMEE VANCE

Revel Books

———

Revel Books
Paperback ISBN: 979-8-9882650-8-5

———

www.aimeevancebooks.com

May the Cove live on forever

Foreword

Thank you so much for joining us again in Deadlights Cove!

While this is a stand-alone, please note that **this story takes place after the end of *Karma is a Witch*** and there may be spoilers for the series as a whole.

Chapter One

CASEY

"Love bites."

I threw myself on the worn couch in Dillon's apartment above Carpe Noctem, staring at the Christmas tree across the room. Something about it seemed off, but maybe that was just my funky mood. *Blue Christmas* churned out on the record player in the corner of the small living room, the perfect vibe for my melancholy statement.

"Sorry, man," Dillon said, running a would-be casual hand through his messy blond hair as his eyes danced between me and the door. "Did something happen?"

"No. That's half the problem though."

Dillon muttered some sort of an assent, his free hand tapping against his leg. Dillon was a drummer in the local band, the Lost Talisman, so the fidgeting wasn't unexpected, but combined with the shifty eyes, I was starting to suspect something was up. The amount of coordinated seasonal decor in his little apartment was surprising, but what did I know. Maybe he was a secret decorator at heart.

Still, something was decidedly different about the apartment since I'd last been here. And that damn tree... I looked back at it and got to my feet, moving to inspect it closer.

"Dude. Did you *measure* the distance between your ornaments?"

"What?" Dillon scoffed, his expression far too dramatic to be normal. "No."

I held out my hands, thumbs touching, to gauge the distance between two, then moved them over to the next branch. "This is way too specific to be accidental." I moved my hands, raising a brow as, once again, the round ornament was perfectly equidistant from the others.

"Can't a guy feel festive this time of year?" Dillon shoved his hands in his pockets, looking at the door for the third time in this short conversation.

I crossed my arms, turning back to the couch that was my new home. Living with my twin brother Cole and his new mate, Skylar, had become painfully awkward once their baby had arrived a few months ago, and it was time to go. I could only take so much of listening to the baby cry, or worse, listening to the two of them go at it.

Usually, renting somewhere in Deadlights Cove wasn't an issue, but there had been shockingly few options when it came time for house hunting.

"You're *sure* I can stay here?" I asked, giving Dillon another out as I crossed the space to the galley kitchen. Everything was color coordinated — strange for a bachelor — but the final nail in the coffin that Dillon no longer lived alone was the inside of his fridge. Clear, neatly stacked containers lined the shelves and there were more vegetables than Dillon had probably eaten in his entire life. I bent over to grab two beers and paused to read the label on a container of lettuce. "Does that say *Romaine Calm?*"

"Yeah." Dillon waved me off, a weird laugh rising out of him. "And I'm positive you can crash here."

I narrowed my eyes as I handed him a beer, my ears pricking up at a noise in the stairwell that he, a witch, wouldn't have heard yet. "Are you absolutely sure there's no one you need to" — a jangle of keys, and the door swung open — "*check* with?"

Kymari stood there, a fluffy cream-color sweater making her dark skin glow as she glanced between Dillon and me.

"Oh, Kymari! Hey!" I feigned shock, throwing Dillon a look that said *Really, dude?*

"Casey, how… unexpected to see you here.". Kymari put her bags down by the door and slipped off her shoes, setting them neatly in the boot tray, and joined us in the living room.

"Dillon was just saying it was absolutely no problem for me to crash here for a bit."

"Hmm."

That was Kymari's response. Dillon grimaced.

Her lips pursed. "How long is *a bit?*"

"Just tonight, right, Case?" Dillon asked, eyes wide.

Well, shit. That hadn't been my plan, but anything was better than listening to my brother bang his mate for the thousandth time.

The three of us entered into a weird stare-off I broke by

taking a long sip of my beer and mumbling an assent. If there was a photo of *Awkward* in the dictionary, it would show us in that living room. Despite the tension we could cut with a knife, I currently had nowhere else to go, so fuck it.

Finding a new place to crash was tomorrow's problem.

———

After a relatively painless evening — thank you, alcohol — Kymari and Dillon retreated to their bedroom, and I pulled off my shirt and traded my jeans for a pair of grey sweatpants, then plopped on the couch. The matching throw pillows didn't fix that this couch was uncomfortable, a hand-me-down from who knew where, the last remnant of Dillon's former bachelorhood.

Once I settled into the least uncomfortable position I could find, I sent a middle-finger selfie to Cole for good measure. Immediately, he sent back a link I knew better than to click — the skulk version of Rick Rolling was *What Does the Fox Say* and I would not give him the satisfaction.

Tossing my phone onto the coffee table, I had just closed my eyes when a series of unmistakable thumps and moans started up from the bedroom. Letting out a frustrated sigh, I stared up at the ceiling, begrudging my singleness yet again.

When all of my friends had been single together, the idea of mating and marriage had seemed so far off, it was hardly a passing thought. But now Kit and Cole were both not only mated but *dads,* and everyone in town seemed to be pairing up.

Nothing made you want a mate to come home to like living in a sex den you reaped no benefits from.

A loud moan punctuated my thoughts, and I ground my teeth together. Sometimes it would be helpful to be able to turn off my fox shifter hearing.

Grabbing two throw pillows, I pressed them against my ears, wishing I hadn't forgotten my earbuds back at my house. Cole's house. Whatever.

I was so distracted trying *not* to hear anything that I almost missed the knocking on the door.

Tossing the pillows aside, I pulled myself to my feet and wrenched open the door, momentarily forgetting this wasn't my apartment.

"If you need Dillon, he's a bit" — I blinked at the woman who stood before me, her honey-brown hair in a long braid over one shoulder under a Lost Talisman beanie — "busy."

Natalie, one of the band's guitarists I'd met in passing a few times, looked me over before peering behind me into the apartment. I took the opportunity to really take her in, and damn, she was gorgeous. Blue eyes, a light dusting of freckles across her nose, and the lean build most shifters had. She was a few inches shorter than me, but just tall enough I wouldn't sprain my neck leaning down to kiss those deep pink, luscious lips I couldn't look away from.

She cleared her throat, and I looked up to meet her mischievous expression as she shared at my bare chest. Natalie was a wolf shifter, not a fox, but same as me, she could not only *hear* what was happening in the apartment behind us, but smell the direction of my dirty thoughts.

I mentally gave myself a cold shower, thinking of rotten vegetables and poopy diapers, both oddly the same color, as Natalie laughed and nudged her way inside.

It took me a minute to realize she was holding a box.

"Here —" I took it from her, a faint hint of her honeysuckle scent reaching me as I drew closer, and my fox urged me to take a deeper sniff, which I ignored. I set the box on the coffee table. "Is this for Dillon?"

"Yeah, band merch. I was going to set up a booth at the holiday craft fair next weekend, but I've been roped into helping Lys with some New Year's Eve party instead so I'm passing it off to Dill," she explained, taking note of the pillows and blanket on the couch. "Are you staying here now? Casey, right?"

I ran a hand through my hair and shrugged. "Just for tonight, then I have to find someplace else."

As she took another step into the apartment, her head tilted, and then she winced, shooting me an apologetic look as she no doubt heard the not-quite-white noise coming from the bedroom.

"Because of that?"

"Not *not* because of that."

She nodded, biting her lip, as though she had something to say but was undecided whether or not to say it.

"Well, as great as this is" — she gestured at the couch, the rattling bedroom door — "if you need somewhere else to crash, it just so happens my roommate moved out recently."

My brows shot up, both excited at the idea of getting the fuck out of here, but also shocked that she'd ask me to move in when we barely knew each other.

"But I'll warn you," she continued, raising an eyebrow, but with a glint in her hazel eyes that told me she was teasing, "if you take me up on the offer, I'll be charging your rent in party help as well as cash."

Just then, the decibel coming from the bedroom ratcheted up, the headboard banging against the wall so hard, the windows in the living room sounded moments away from shattering.

I pulled on my shirt, jacket, shoes, and grabbed my bag before she could change her mind.

"Lead the way."

Chapter Two

NATALIE

Had I really just invited a total stranger to come live with me? I barely made it down Dillon's stairs without tripping, I was so discombobulated. But the heavy steps of Casey's boots behind me told me that indeed I had.

Okay, it wasn't like he was an axe murderer or something. I knew him, sort of — knew *of* him, really, but in a small town like the Cove, the two went hand in hand. I'd never heard anything bad about Casey, aside from the typical "menace to society" label most fox shifters toted.

For the last two years, I'd lived in my small house on pack lands with my cousin Sierra until she'd up and moved to Alaska, of all places. While my mortgage wasn't terrible thanks to the deal Darius, our pack Alpha, had cut me, I'd always had Sierra's rent money coming in. I hadn't worried too much about it before she moved out, but Lys had booked us for fewer shows than usual this year with his increasing responsibilities to the Coven, and suddenly I was hurting for cash.

There was also a very real possibility my brain had short-circuited seeing Casey shirtless, with his swirling skulk tattoos on full display. His shaggy dark hair and that sly smirk so typical of fox shifters hadn't hurt either. My wolf had perked right up at his pine and citrus scent, ready to roll in the snow with him. Within seconds of being in his presence, she was all in on anything that included spending more time with Casey, especially if he walked around semi-nude regularly.

Not that I was planning on sleeping with him.

Crap, was I? No.

That was just the lingering scent of sex in the air, wafting from the apartment behind us and derailing my train of thought. It was cruel to leave a shifter subject to the noises and scents in that apartment, something pea-brained Dillon wouldn't understand. Kymari did though. Maybe this was her insurance policy to make sure Casey wouldn't overstay his one-night welcome.

"Where exactly do you live?" Casey asked as he opened the exterior door, a rush of cold air greeting us as we headed out onto the snow-covered sidewalk. "I probably should have asked that already."

"Pack lands," I answered, then stopped. Casey slammed into my back with an *oof*, his hands automatically cupping my arms to steady us, as I looked over my shoulder at him. Even that small touch through several layers of clothing was enough to have all of my nerves alight, but I willed my horny wolf to calm down. *Rent money*, I chanted to myself, then stepped away from him. "You're aware you have to behave, right? If Darius catches wind I let you stay on pack lands and then you go and stir up shit, you're going to put me in a difficult position with the pack."

Casey held up a hand in a pledge. "Best behavior."

I squinted, the brisk air cutting through the hazy thoughts my mind had been in a few minutes ago. "Maybe this was a bad idea. Aren't you the one who filled pack cars with shaving cream that one year?"

Casey smirked, snow catching on his dark hair and eyelashes. Between his roguish expression and the memory of how amazing his body had looked when he'd opened the door, I could hardly think straight. "I can neither confirm nor deny those allegations."

I snorted, then crossed the street to my car. Casey followed behind, folding his tall frame into my van. It wasn't glamorous, but I'd retrofitted the back seats to fit dog crates.

A fact Casey took in with a bemused expression. "Don't tell me you're making coats in your free time, Cruella. Wait, am I being kidnapped? Oh shit, I just got in a stranger's van, and you didn't even offer me candy!"

Rolling my eyes, I pulled into the street and started out of the square, towards pack lands. "My day job is as a dog trainer. Some clients have me pick up their dogs for trail runs or overnight stays, and I want to make sure everyone's safe back there while we're driving."

"Huh. Is that cheating on the dog training thing since you're a wolf?"

"It's not cheating, it's *smart*. I make great money doing

this, and it gives me the flexibility to play in as many festivals and bars as Lys books us, which is what I love doing most. Plus, it saves a lot of dogs from being put down just because their dumbass humans didn't know how to communicate with them."

Casey chuckled, the low rumble of it making me all too aware of his proximity. "Noted."

Needing to change the subject, I switched on the radio. "What kind of music do you like?"

"You know Ed Sheeran?"

"Hilarious."

Casey grinned, blue eyes dancing, and goddamn. This fox may be the death of me.

———

Crossing into pack lands a few minutes later, Casey straightened in his seat, whether from noticing the scent markings or from some sensation of the magic in the border.

"Ever been on pack lands before?"

"Officially, no," he said, tapping his fingers on his jeans. "Maybe once or twice unofficially, but a fox never pranks and tells. Ever been on skulk lands?"

I shook my head. "I've only seen photos, like the ones Nimue sometimes sells at the craft fairs. It's beautiful. Pack lands are pretty similar — I think our range is less hilly than yours, but we like to keep our houses spread out. Room to run between us."

My mailbox came into view, and I suddenly felt nervous

at showing Casey my home, even though that was dumb. It was better than Dillon's couch, at least.

"I bought the house a few years ago in a rent-to-buy deal from Darius," I offered, attempting to break some of the tension.

It was an old green Maine cabin, with a big deck out front and an A-line roof on the second floor. I'd added a large, fenced in area for the dogs I boarded out back, but other than that, I hadn't made many additions, and the whole place was pretty rustic.

I parked the van, and Casey grabbed his bag and followed me inside.

A pellet stove stood to the right, which was the first thing I checked, refilling the hopper and making sure it was set for the night. Luckily, with such a small house, it didn't take much to heat it. Across from the stove was a couch, and behind that, the kitchen. The spare bedroom was off the back of that, and my room was upstairs.

"Your room is down the hall," I said, pointing, and Casey nodded, heading back to it. "It's furnished, and there should be some spare sheets in the linen closet next to the bathroom. Want a beer?"

It was late, but what the hell. I didn't have any clients tomorrow until the afternoon, and Casey didn't strike me as an early bird either.

"Sure," he called from the room, and I pulled two from the fridge. And some popcorn that I tossed in the microwave.

I was setting everything on the coffee table in the living room when Casey rejoined me, laptop open in his hands.

"Hey, what's your WiFi password?"

I opened my mouth to reply, but at that moment, he looked at me over the top of his laptop, and no sound came out.

Why the fuck did the sight of him in glasses make me forget how to brain words?

Chapter Three

CASEY

N atalie stared at me, beer halfway to her slightly parted lips. I looked down, making sure I hadn't spilled anything on myself. But, I couldn't have, because I hadn't had anything to eat or drink yet since we got here. Get it together, Case.

"Um, Nat? Password?"

She blinked, shaking her head as I sat down next to her on the couch, propping my laptop on the coffee table. "Right. It's" — she reached to the side of the couch, procuring a sticky note and passing it to me — "here."

I took the sticky note, read it, then furrowed my brow. "Is this a joke? Your password is bigbadwolf1?"

She took a long swig of her beer and shrugged. "Yeah, so?"

I scoffed, typing in the password and getting connected. "Okay, well that's going to change. I don't even need to huff *or* puff to blow this firewall down."

In seconds, I was navigating to up the security of her

WiFi, ignoring her protests in the background until they faded away. Until —

"You wear glasses?"

"Huh?" Her words registered a second later, and I glanced over at her, still typing. "Oh, blue light. Sometimes I get a headache if I code too long."

She gripped the neck of her beer, reminding me I had one waiting for me too. I swiped it off the table and clinked it to hers.

"Cheers, roomie."

"Cheers."

Then I choked mid-sip at the results that popped up on my computer. "*This* is your WiFi speed?" I turned the screen for her to see, my knee brushing hers in the process. I tried not to register the shiver of electricity that mild contact ignited in me, focusing instead on the dire circumstances at hand. "Do you even use the internet?"

She *shrugged*. "Not really. Just for booking clients, and sometimes band stuff. Once in a while my cousin and I would watch a movie, but there are always DVDs and cable TV."

I tilted my head back, letting out a long breath. "Okay. Okay, it's fixable. Not tonight, but it's fine."

Natalie laughed. "What's the big deal?"

I shut my laptop as a lost cause and settled back onto the couch, helping myself to a handful of popcorn and chucking one at her nose. "The *big deal* is I need it for work. And also, you know, to live in the twenty-first century."

"Whatever, nerd," she teased, but her smile told me it wasn't meant as a dig. "What do you do for work?"

I nodded my beer at my laptop. "I'm a full stack developer."

"I have not the slightest clue what that means."

"You and just about everyone else." I sipped my beer. "Pretty much anything with computer code, I can do it."

"So, you could make me a new website?"

"Easy. And Cole can make it look great — he's a graphic designer. Is that part of the rent?"

"Let's call it the security deposit."

"Done." I held out my hand to shake on it, which turned out to be a mistake. Her small, warm palm met mine, and suddenly, I wanted to know what all of her skin felt like. If it was all as smooth as the soft skin of the underside of her wrist I hadn't meant to brush. I dropped her hand before I could start caressing her wrist like a freak and cleared my throat. "By the way, what is the rent?"

If Nat was as affected by our handshake as I was, she hid it better than I did, explaining the details of the rental agreement without any sign she wanted to feel up the rest of *my* skin.

"Does that sound good?"

Skin. What? "Sure."

I had no idea what I just agreed to, but it would probably be fine. My business had been lucrative for years now. It wasn't that I couldn't afford to live alone, I just didn't *like* to. I blamed being a twin — I'd never been alone, not even in the womb.

"I would ask to see your current website, but I'm not sure your internet can handle it."

Rolling her eyes again, Nat gestured for me to reopen

my laptop, and when I did, she typed the address into the browser. I pretended to check my watch as we waited for the page to load, and she elbowed me in the ribs.

"Oh, boy," I whistled, scrolling through her page. It was beyond outdated, the formatting horrible, and half her links didn't even work. "You actually book clients through this?"

"Hey, it's not that bad. But usually, no. Most of my business is by word-of-mouth, I just keep a website to look legit if anyone looks me up."

I was skimming her reviews — that page did link correctly to publicly posted search engine reviews — when one caught my eye. Frowning, I put my beer down, pulling my computer onto my lap to look more closely.

"Oh, don't —" Nat reached for my computer, trying to close it, but I held it out of her reach.

"What the hell is this?"

Nat slumped back on the couch. "Disgruntled customer. It's nothing, really. He had a dog — a husky — that he really didn't have the lifestyle for. The dog was super high energy, needed a lot of exercise and stimulation, and this guy spends most of his days watching golf. Anyway, I suggested to him that he might not be the best fit for that dog and that I'd be happy to work with him on rehoming her, and he freaked out. Now he leaves me bad reviews everywhere my business is listed. I think he might be making new accounts to leave me reviews too, since he's the only person I've ever suggested rehoming a dog to."

I frowned, but set my laptop back on the coffee table. "That's pretty shitty."

Nat lifted a shoulder. "The occasional bad review is a

part of any business. It's fine. Eventually, he'll find someone else to pester."

I hummed, staring at the screen for another moment before shutting my laptop. She didn't ask me to do anything about it, so I wouldn't. Not now, at least.

"Well." I sipped my beer, then stretched my arm across the back of the couch, resisting the temptation to run my fingers across her golden braid. "Show me what life is like in the Dark Ages, Nat. Pop in a DVD."

Chapter Four

NATALIE

A steady buzzing woke me up the next morning, my phone vibrating across the wood nightstand. I groaned, shoving my pillow over my head as I waited for whoever had the audacity to call this early to leave a message. My voicemail clearly stated my business hours were 10-4, and it was nowhere near 10 a.m. yet. It wasn't even light out yet, for crying out loud.

I breathed a sigh of relief when the vibrating stopped, but the joke was on me, because it just started up again immediately after.

Flipping over my phone, I squinted at the screen, grumbling at the name flashing across it.

"Do you have any idea what time it is?" I croaked after I'd answered the call.

"It's five minutes *after* Lysander had agreed to meet with us to discuss our vision of the event," came Val's voice. "And as Lys's replacement, you should be here by now."

"I'm already regretting agreeing to this," I muttered.

"We heard that."

"Well I said it into the phone," I sniped back, crabby before my morning coffee, not to mention the other three hours of sleep I'd planned on, then took a breath. "Sorry. Okay. I'll be there as soon as I can."

"Lovely."

I hung up, then threw my phone onto the bed. But, I had agreed to help and I tried to be a wolf of my word, so after a thirty-second pity party, I hauled myself out of bed.

On my way to the bathroom for a quick shower, I knocked on Casey's door, the wood creaking open on the hinges.

"Hey, the guys just called. They want to meet us to go over — oh —" I choked over the rest of my words as Casey's fully nude body came into sight, passed out on the bed. Toned legs gave way to just about the nicest ass I'd ever seen as the sheet draped just right over his lower body.

His head lifted just barely, cracking one eye open at me.

"So, you're naked." Great observation, Nat. We were shifters, it wasn't a big deal. *Shouldn't* have been a big deal. Should not have made saliva gather in my mouth. And yet —

"Oh, my God, I am. You *are* trying to steal my pelt! I knew it! Cruella!"

How he could go from dead asleep to smartass in ten seconds flat, I had no idea, but I clicked his door shut and ran for the bathroom, hoping I'd left before he had a chance to scent anything that view might have done to me.

I could *not* have feelings for my roommate. No matter how fine his ass was.

———

A half-hour later, we were back in my van and fully clothed, heading into town. I refused to acknowledge the shit-eating grin on Casey's face, keeping my eyes glued to the road.

"Wanna talk about it?" Casey said.

I side-eyed him. "Nope."

"You stared at my ass."

"I said I *didn't* want to talk about it."

"I have a pretty nice ass," Casey went on. "Can't really blame you for staring."

"Do you always sleep naked?"

His brows rose, that stupid smirk he wore so often creeping up. "Why? Wondering if you'll get a sneak peek of anything… *else?* You could just ask nicely and I'll show you whatever you want."

A high-pitched laugh escaped me before I could stop it. I was in a band with three guys and spent most of my time in bars — I was used to forward advances. I was even *more* used to turning them down. So what was it about Casey that left me tongue-tied?

My wolf panted, ready to jump at his offer, but I shoved her down in my consciousness, refusing to give in to her lust. "We're roommates. That would be a terrible idea."

He shrugged. "I don't know. We're adults. Maybe it's convenient, not terrible."

"Your brain has been addled from listening to people bone all night, every night."

Casey chuckled, tilting his head back to rest on the seat. "It's definitely messed with me." He tipped his head to the side, blue eyes steady on me. "I should have asked this before now, but any jealous boyfriends I need to be leary of? Is somebody going to come home while I'm minding my own business, sleeping in the nude, and fill my truck with shaving cream as a claim on you?"

"Definitely not."

He was quiet for so long, I peeked a glance at him, catching those dark brows raised in question once more.

"That's a pretty firm answer you gave there. Is it story time?"

"No story. I just don't have time to date between running my own business and band gigs."

"So that means you need a frenefits situation."

"I need *no* situation, is what it means."

Casey shrugged, whistling along to the radio.

"Can we not make this a thing between us?" I asked, chewing my lip as I worried over the state of living with someone I was this attracted to. It hadn't even been a full 24 hours, and already I was cursing myself for agreeing to this, rent money be damned. "Let's forget the whole thing happened. I saw nothing."

He frowned, looking back over at me as we parked in front of Scallywags. "I didn't mean to make you uncomfortable, Natalie. I took it too far, but I'm not an ass, I promise. I won't mention it again, if that's what you want. And I swear all my manly bits will be fully covered in any common areas, like a good roommate."

I nodded, hearing the sincerity in his words. "Good." Shoving the door open a little too hard, I jumped out of the van, landing in ankle-deep snow as I tried to convince myself that *was* what I wanted. Wasn't it?

Casey walked in front of me to pull open the door to Scallywags, and the sight of his jeans-clad ass made me second guess myself.

"Tacky Christmas is overdone," Val said as we stepped inside. "Everyone does that. And who decides what's tacky and what's not?"

"That Edward Cullen sweater is pretty tacky," Casey whispered in my ear as we settled at the bar. As they did every year, Val and Caedmon wore their Christmas *Twilight* sweaters — one with a giant, sparkling Edward Cullen face, the other with Jacob. I held back a smile, taking in the rest of the room.

Most of the chairs were up on the tables, put away from the night before, except for the few occupied by the other volunteers. Blaze, the bar owner, sat sprawled in a chair next to Morgaine, an elderly witch who was always involved in everything around town. At the table next to them were Peg Fernsby and Eva Watford, the Historical Society witches, and the mayor Orion leaned against the wall, white angel wings hanging loose behind him.

"What about another Bake Off?" Peg offered, and Caedmon scoffed.

"We did that *last* year. Don't you think it's time for new ideas?"

"You've done the Bake Off *multiple* years in a row. Why are we breaking tradition now?" Eva butted in. "I had my recipes all lined up. Everyone in town was looking forward to it."

"No one was looking forward to her dry fruit cake, trust me," Cascy whispered again, and I smacked him in the stomach, thankful we were the only shifters in the room.

"It's time we think of more than just ourselves." Val held his hands out to the side, as if he was addressing a packed theater rather than the six of us trying not to fall asleep in an empty bar at seven in the morning. "The holiday season is about giving back, giving to those less fortunate, providing for those in need."

Blaze picked up the paper on the table in front of him, brow furrowed as he read it, then glanced up. "Explain to me how *Winston* is less fortunate? He's a moose whose diet consists of pink frosted donuts, provided free of charge."

Caedmon scoffed, a hand over his heart. "We've encroached on his territory, taken over his homeland, ruined his chances of procreating. Pink donuts are the *least* we can do for our loyal friend."

"And isn't it magical that love blooms even still?"

Orion sighed, rubbing the bridge of his nose. "Bagheera is a *cat*. My cat, that lives in my house." He waved the flyer in the air, fingers crumpling the paper. "He doesn't need a *love nest* with his moose friend."

"I think you mean his moose *lover*, O," Blaze chided, and Orion shot him a look to kill.

"Let's move this along, boys," Morgaine said, trying to refocus the group. "What's the theme for the party?"

"Enchanted Masquerade," Val breathed, beaming.

"Masquerade? In a town where everyone knows everyone and half of them are shifters who could scent everyone identity from across the — *oof* —"

Orion's critiques were cut off by a sharp elbow to the kidney, courtesy of Peg Fernsby.

"I think it's a *fabulous* idea," she breathed, patting Orion's shoulder as the mayor clutched his side, doubling over. "Sequins, gowns, dark corners," her hand fluttered over her chest, "secret lovers, clandestine trysts, bodices *ripped* in the heat of —"

"Yes, well," Caedmon interrupted her with a frown. "Something like that, anyway."

"Fog machines?" Peg's eyes glittered with a ferocity just shy of manic.

Caedmon and Val exchanged a glance, and Val lifted a shoulder.

"Say no more, gentlemen." Peg was out the door before the guys were quite sure what they'd even agreed to, apparently off to hunt down a fog machine.

"Food?" Eva asked, tapping her pen on the notepad in front of her.

"I can get bar food. Bring out the cotton candy machine," Blaze said, and Val cringed.

"Leave it to me, boys," Eva said. "I'll be in charge of the food. This is a classy affair."

"That's going to be *in a bar*," Blaze raised a brow.

"Yes, yes." Caedmon waved his hand in Blaze's direction. "Thank you so much for volunteering to host it, Sabazios. If you wouldn't mind being in charge of alcohol, that would be lovely. And Orion, can you spread the word about the fundraiser through the town's messaging system? We have three weeks to get this right, and we'll need all of the ticket sales we can get to raise enough money for

25

Winston's new barn."

Blaze pushed back from his table, heading to his office in the back. Orion heaved a sigh and shook his head as he walked out the front doors, headed towards town hall.

"Now"— Caedmon clapped his hands together, turning to us at last — "Decor."

"I'll share my vision board with you," Val offered, tapping away on his tablet as the guys joined us over at the bar counter. "At all times, remember the *vision*. What's your email, Nat?"

I semi-reluctantly gave him my email, my phone pinging with his notification a second later. I hesitantly pulled it out of my pocket. "Lys was really going to do *all* the decorations?"

"He was," Caedmon confirmed. "And without complaint." He raised a bushy white brow.

"For Winston, Nat," Casey admonished, swiping my phone before I could stop him and going straight to the link Val had sent and letting out a whistle. "Wow, man. This is —"

"Spectacular? Bewitching? Yes, I know," Val giggled, and twined his arms around Caedmon's. "It was inspired by the night we met."

"Oh?" Casey's eyebrows disappeared into his hairline.

"Not now, Valerian," Caedmon murmured, patting Val's hand. "Save it for the party." Turning to us, he added, "He's working on a theatrical retelling."

"Remember the doublet you wore that night?" Val said wistfully, his hands sliding down Caedmon's back. "So handsome."

"Well, personally, I can't wait." Casey jerked his head emphatically, tugging me towards the door with him as the two men started nuzzling. Anyone who had been in the Cove for any length of time knew it was only a matter of seconds before these two were packing on the PDA. "Better get going if we're going to make this vision come to life."

Once outside, I let out the groan I'd been holding in. "Oh, I'm going to kill Lys."

Casey chuckled as we trudged back towards my van, snow crunching under our boots. "How exactly did you get roped into doing this for him?"

"He agreed to help out as a favor to the guys, then remembered, oh wait, he's head of everything now and doesn't have time to plan parties. Enter me being an absolute sap and saying I'd do it for him when he was spiraling. But in my defense, he made it sound way less intense than all that." I gestured back towards Scallywags. "I thought I needed to run to a party store and pick up an order, not *this*."

"So Lys isn't helping at all now?"

"No. Maisie whisked him away on a belated honeymoon to get away from Coven pressure. They won't be back until after the new year."

"Well," Casey said as he draped his arm over my shoulder, sending a tingly zing up my spine. My stomach fluttered at all his warmth pressing up to me, his pine and citrus scent overwhelming me, and my wolf practically started panting for him. "Lucky for you, I'm here to help."

He dropped his arm and hopped in the van while I

stood outside, snow falling steadily as I forced myself to let the heat from his touch dissipate.

I needed to get my head on straight if I was going to keep this distance between us. Anything *more* with Casey was a no — it couldn't happen. He was my roommate, and maybe a friend. That was enough.

Wasn't it?

Chapter Five

CASEY

Over the next week, I moved more of my stuff in from Cole's house and upgraded Nat's internet to a usable, 21st century speed. Living on pack lands was strange, and I got more than a few odd looks as I drove by in my 1984 Ford F-150 truck on the way to and from the house, but whether that was because I was a fox, or because of its rust spots and rumbling engine was hard to say. I'd intended on fixing the exterior as much as I'd redone the engine, but I kind of loved the sideways glances I earned every time I drove by in the big rust bucket.

Luckily, the pack and the skulk were on good terms lately, so as long as I kept my snout clean, they shouldn't have a problem with me being here.

The downside to living way out in the middle of nowhere with semi-unreliable internet was that sometimes, I didn't know what to fucking do with myself. Before Cole and Skylar mated, a whole gang of us had lived in the house together, and there was always someone to hang out with. I'd rocked my third wheel status even after everyone else moved out, refusing to leave my brother's and my house for as long as possible. T Arrietty arrived, and with a baby in the house, everything changed. As much as I loved my brother, I knew I'd overstayed my welcome.

I was unused to silence. Between band practice and her business, Natalie was gone a lot, and I was home alone for the first time in a long time. Cole and I had both worked from home for years, sharing a crowded office space, and I missed my brother something fierce.

I'd assembled my desk first, crowded with monitors to make work easier. Rainbow LEDs glowed from the keyboard and the computer I built myself, but even though my setup was the same, it all felt lonely here. I had no one to shoot the shit with while I worked, and I didn't realize until now how much I counted on Cole's constant banter to get me through the day.

When it took an hour for systems to spin up on this archaic network, I was crawling out of my skin. Even with the upgraded internet speed, it wasn't enough to run my programs *and* stream shows, so I started finding other things to do.

One day I fixed the wiring to the light over the kitchen sink so we could actually use it. The next, I tackled the closet door in my room — more of a closet *panel* since it just sat there, no hinges — installing it properly. Another, I was taking a walk around the house for a break, and noticed one of the dogs must have tried to dig its way to freedom, so I filled in the holes at the fenceline.

Leaky faucet? Fixed. Creaky door? Oiled. Hole in the wall? Patched and painted.

Pretty soon I would run out of things to fix in Natalie's small house, but I'd cross that bridge when I came to it. Technically, I could work on decorations for the masquerade without her, but it had become a ritual for us to work on them together every night, and I needed that little dose of routine and companionship. Chatting over paper chains and hot glue guns had become the highlight of my day. I hardly recognized myself.

"Hey," Nat called out as she came in on my sixth day with her, sounding dead beat. "Do you want to order takeout?"

"Sure," I called back from my room, finishing up for the night myself. The sound of her hopping up the stairs to her room was a balm for my sad, lonely soul. The degree to which my fox perked up at another living soul being around was a little pathetic.

I powered down my PC to go meet her in the kitchen, beer at the ready. Leaning on the kitchen island, I pulled out my phone to text Blaze our order from Scallywags.

Footsteps on the stairs again signaled Natalie returning. "Ugh, I'd give anything to take a bath tonight. The dog I worked with today was a puller, and at 120 pounds, my shoulder is done."

"Why can't you take a bath?"

"Drain's busted."

"Fixed that. Burgers?" I asked, thumbs hovering over my phone.

"What?"

"Or would you rather the chicken sandwich? Rosemary fries are an obvious yes."

"No, you fixed the drain?" Her hand landed on my forearm, drawing my eyes up to her.

Her golden-brown hair was loose around her shoulders, slightly messy from hat-head after a long day outside in the cold. In just an oversized Lost Talisman tee, boyshorts that showed off her toned legs, and knee-high socks, she'd never looked sexier. My traitorous eyes dropped as my mouth went dry, and fuck me. She wasn't wearing a bra.

Her fingers tapped my forearm. "What?" I blinked at her stupidly.

"The drain?" She tilted her head, her silky hair cascading with the motion, and damn, I wanted to reach out and feel it.

"Yeah." I straightened up, then winced as the motion caused friction in places that did *not* need to be encouraged, and plopped down on the stool next to me. "It was clogged, and you needed a new stopper. No biggie."

"*Yes*, biggie!" She squealed, looping her arms around my neck in a quick hug with a peck to the cheek, her honeysuckle scent enveloping me. My skin tingled where her lips brushed it. And now I wanted them everywhere. "I've been wanting to get that fixed since I bought the place but never got around to it. Okay, dinner's on me, cash is in my purse. I'm going to take a *bath*" — she sighed happily over the word — "then let's watch a movie while we make some decorations."

She took off for the bathroom, which was for the best.

"Sounds good," I said, my voice barely a croak, and I adjusted my pants with a hiss. My fingertips traced my cheek.

She'd set a pretty firm boundary about sleeping together, which was fine, of course. And she had on far more clothes tonight than I had that first morning.

Did it still count if I just thought of her while I rubbed one out?

Shit.

————

I paced my room the entire time she was in the bath, doing my best not to picture her in there. Then I switched my jeans for sweatpants. Would looser fabric be better? I wasn't sure, but I knew I needed less friction or I was going to combust.

The doorbell rang with the food, and I let out a breath, meeting my own eye in my closet mirror.

"You can do this, Case." I wished I believed me.

An unhappy Nox stood in the gathering snow with our bag of food, the PopNox delivery van idling in the driveway. It had been snowing off and on all week, but tonight it was coming down in heavy sheets, almost a white out. "Blaze has you on delivery service tonight, Fireball?"

"Just take your food. Snow might be worse than rain."

I chuckled, handing the demon an extra tip, and he sprinted back to his van without another word.

Snow swirled around the porch as I closed the door, the

33

smell of rosemary fries almost distracting me from thoughts of a naked Natalie down the hall.

Almost.

I set the bag on the coffee table before grabbing plates, napkins, and fresh beers for us.

Nat emerged with a cloud of lavender-scented steam a moment later, a serene smile on her glowing face. She was back in the oversized tee, boyshorts, and knee socks, wet hair cascading down her back. And I was back to hiding my boner.

"Better?" I popped the bottle caps, handing her one as she sat beside me, long legs pulled up on the couch as she sat with her feet to the side. Her knees grazed my thigh, and just that bare contact was enough to have me closing my eyes, reaching for every ounce of willpower I had.

"Much. Cheers to my live-in handyman." She grinned, clinking her bottle to mine and taking a long swig I watched intently. "Did you pick a movie?"

I forced myself to look away from her, nodding to her meager stack of DVDs by the television. "From your collection of five?"

"Or you could show me that fancy 'streaming' you always talk about."

"No thanks. Life's too short for buffering."

"You fixed the internet!"

I shook my head. "Barely. Maybe enough for 1080p on a good day, but once you've seen 4k, you can't go back."

Nat narrowed her eyes at me as she pulled out a handful of fries. "Sometimes I think you just make this stuff up."

I rolled my eyes. Maybe one day, she'd see the light.

"Okay, so of my *eight* DVDs, what's your pick?"

"Surprise me."

Letting out what could only be described as a maniacal cackle, Nat leapt off the couch and ran over to the DVDs, not letting me see which one she picked. She bent over to put it in the player, and I had to close my eyes, knowing the change in my scent would give me away anyway.

She'd asked me to stay away though, so I wasn't going to mention it again unless she did, even if we both knew the direction of my thoughts.

The opening credits ran, and I gave a resigned nod as I started on my burger. "Legally Blonde. Classic. Did you pick this one because you thought it would annoy me the most?"

Nat tilted her head, hand on her popped hip. "What, like it's hard?"

I moved my plate over my lap. *Something* was hard, I had to give her that.

While the movie played, Natalie fetched our crafting supplies, putting them on the coffee table in front of us with instructions for tonight's craft.

I cut mindlessly, not hearing the movie besides the sound of Nat's laugh. She smiled, mouthing quotes she knew well, and I couldn't stop my mind from fixating on how badly I wanted her.

How had we been in the same town, running in the same circles, for this long, and I'd never noticed her before? I certainly was now.

It wasn't even just her stunning looks that captivated me. She had a carefree attitude paired with a drive that led her to burn the candle at both ends, doing what she loved both with animals and her band. Not only did I respect the hell out of that, I saw that same drive in myself.

"I'm starting to think you aren't taking this seriously, Case." Natalie raised a brow at the paper chain I was busy making. About the hundredth one tonight.

"How can you say that to me?" I dropped my scissors, holding up my hand. "You see these? Scissor blisters. I'm wounding myself for my art right now."

"We agreed on a snowflake design. This looks —"

"Way better than snowflakes."

She held up my paper chain, stretching it out to see the design, and frowned.

"Casey."

"Natalie."

"Am I mistaken, or are these penises?"

I tilted my head, squinting at them, barely hiding my smile. "Huh. Are they?"

"Casey!" She hurled the paper at me, then started shuffling through the rest of my stacks of paper chains. "Bruiser Woods, are they *all* penises?"

I shrugged. "Val clearly said the night is inspired by the night he met Caedmon, so if you think about it —"

She shoved the paper chain in my mouth to shut me up. I blew it back out.

"— I'm just staying true to the spirit of the event," I finished as though nothing had happened, then lowered my voice. "But hey, if you wanted to see me with a dick in my mouth, you need only ask. I've never done that before, but whatever floats your boat, Nat. But" — I held up my hands — "we made very strict rules about that kind of thing, and I am honor bound to keep them."

She sighed, closing her eyes against dealing with me. "I need another drink."

Chapter Six

NATALIE

NATALIE

The male is in grey sweatpants. Grey! Sweatpants!

DILLON

So?

BODHI

Get it, girl.

NATALIE

You guys are useless.

BODHI

What's the problem?

NATALIE

Uhh, we're roommates? It would be a bad idea to mix business with pleasure.

BODHI

Since when?

DILLON

Wait, should I buy grey sweatpants? Is this like a sex thing?

LYS

Yes, it's a thing, Dill. Buy some. Thank us later.

I sat on the edge of the tub, chewing my thumb nail as I thought through the last week with Casey. Even before tonight, he hadn't done much to hide his interest in me, although he'd held good to his word not to push me.

Something was different tonight, though. Maybe it was just the bath, or the numerous other things I'd noticed he'd fixed this week, but I felt good about him being here, comfortable in my own house. If he could walk around shirtless, then I could walk around pantsless, right? My wolf said yes, but she was a horny bitch, so maybe I should have thought this through more.

The light above the sink flickered, then went out, plunging me into darkness. Luckily, with my shifter eyesight and the light of my phone, I could see easily enough even though there was no window for natural light in the bathroom.

NATALIE

I think our power just went out.

BODHI

How romantic! It's a sign.

NATALIE

You really are the demon on my shoulder.

BODHI

I will not apologize.

Clicking off my phone, I sucked in a deep breath for courage and went to face the music.

I wanted Casey. And now, by the looks of things, we were about to be snowed in. Deadlights Cove was notorious for power outages in big storms, much to Orion's chagrin, but even more so on remote pack lands.

Was Bodhi right? Was this a sign from the universe?

"Do you have flashlights around here?" Casey asked, the pellet stove casting his face in sharp shadows, highlighting the angles of his cheekbones and the line of his jaw. A jaw I suddenly had the desperate desire to lick.

"Uhh, yes, hang on." Tearing my eyes away from him, I rummaged in the 'everything' kitchen drawer, finding a small emergency flashlight and a headlamp.

I turned to set them on the kitchen island, nearly dropping them when I bumped right into Casey.

He chuckled, steadying me, and took both items from my hands, testing them out.

The flashlight clicked uselessly, the batteries dead. The headlamp gave a faint glow, but hardly better than our shifter sight already allowed.

"Well, maybe we're done with scissors or anything potentially hazardous in the dark for the night," he said, setting them down on the counter.

The wind howled as the storm kicked up, rattling the windows in the dark living room. I leaned against the counter, my heartbeat nearly drowning out the wind as I stared at Casey's chest, trying to find the courage to make a move.

Since we were both shifters, he could scent the direction of my thoughts just as easily as I could smell his interest, as evidenced by his widening pupils. My fists clenched at my sides as I hesitated, the few feet between us seeming like miles. I wasn't shy, wasn't a virgin, but I also wasn't used to being the pursuer. And I'd drawn this line in the sand between us — he'd just reminded me of that minutes ago.

"Nat," Casey's voice was low, and he stepped closer. His eyes flashed to the gold of his fox then back to blue.

"This is a bad idea," I breathed, trying to convince myself to walk away. Trying to convince myself not to. My wolf urged me forward, zero hesitation on her end, but I still wavered.

Casey stopped, leaving space between us as he nodded. His jaw worked, drawing my eyes to his lips, imagining what they would feel like against my skin.

He cleared his throat. "I can go to my room."

My eyes snapped up, and my determination slammed down.

In an instant, I reached for him, my fingers tangling in the soft fabric of his tee, pulling him towards me. Without missing a beat, Casey's head tipped down, his mouth finding mine in the near darkness like we'd done this a thousand times. His hands settled on my waist, clutching me to him, electricity shooting down my spine at his hands on me, his skin on mine. I could hardly stand upright.

Like he could read my mind, my feet left the ground, and he sat me on the counter, pushing between my knees and leaning into me. My lips parted instinctively, and Casey's tongue swiped in, tangling with mine. He tugged me closer to the edge of the counter, a groan slipping from him as he pressed himself against me.

How had I waited a week to feel his touch? How had I turned *this* down?

I looped my arms around his neck, fingers tangling in his messy hair as we kissed like our lives depended on it, his devouring leaving me breathless. His hand skimmed under my shirt, pausing to see if I would stop him, then skated up my ribs until he cupped my breast, giving my nipple a pinch sharp enough to draw a gasp from me as he lowered his lips to my ear.

"Were you trying to torture me coming downstairs like this?"

I smiled, words lost to me, but ground my hips against his hardness in answer.

"I'm never going to be able to eat in this kitchen again without picturing you grinding down on me, just like this."

Pulling his face back to mine, I kissed him again, giving in to the fire pulsing in my veins. While I'd been attracted to him from the moment he answered Dillon's door, this felt... more. More than just physical attraction. It was like

I'd waited my whole life for Casey, and that was ridiculous. We'd known each other for a week. This had to just be sexual tension driving us both.

"Why do I feel like I'm going to die if I can't feel all of you?" Casey mirrored my thoughts, his hands tightening on my waist as he hovered his mouth above mine, sharing air.

Rather than answer, I grabbed the hem of his shirt and lifted it over his head, needing his skin on mine. My fingers raked over his chest, the same lean muscles etched in my brain from that first day, but touching them was so much better than seeing them. He swallowed heavily as he studied me studying him, his heart beating as wildly as mine.

"Off." Casey pulled on my shirt, discarding it too. The moment I was free of it, he pulled me to his chest, plastering us together and crashing his mouth back down on mine. My legs tangled around his hips, letting him move me closer to slide his hands beneath my ass and lift me. We fumbled down the hallway towards his room, darkness enveloping us as he dropped me to the bed, covering me with his body in the next instant.

His scent was all over his bed, and it took everything in my power not to shove my nose into his pillow and inhale him. Something about it, being in his bed, surrounded by his woodsy scent, the blanket of darkness — I'd never felt so safe.

"Birth control?"

A breath escaped me as his teeth found the skin just above my breast, and I struggled to maintain a coherent thought to answer him.

"Yes."

43

His mouth lifted off me a second before he tugged my boyshorts off, bending my knees and settling between my thighs.

"Last chance, Nat," Casey groaned as his hands found their way between my legs, rubbing me in all the best ways.

"If you stop now, I'll sic the entire pack on you."

His teeth flashed in the scant moonlight streaming in from outside, grinning as he nipped my inner thigh.

"Yes, ma'am."

Then his tongue traced over me, and my head thumped back into my pillow. A moan escaped him, and his hands cupped my ass, tugging me into his face more firmly.

"Goddamn, Nat," was all he could get out, and I wasn't faring much better. Maybe it was the snowstorm, or a competency kink after he'd fixed so much stuff around the house, but I'd never felt need like this before.

My back arched off the bed, and when he slid two fingers inside me, I tangled my hands in his hair. I bucked my hips, earning me another groan from him, and he met my rhythm, building up the coiling tension inside me.

The moment he sucked on me and curled his fingers just right, I shattered.

"Case," I managed to breathe as he worked me through it, lifting his head to give me a smug grin.

His blue eyes were rimmed in gold, the line between his fox and himself paper thin, but I was positive I looked the same. My wolf shared in my excitement, feeling this connection just as much as I did.

Casey crawled over me, kissing his way back up my

body until his hips settled over mine. I gripped his face, kissing him hard, wanting to show him how much I wanted this. Wanted him.

"You're the best thing I've ever fucking tasted," he murmured, his lips moving to my neck, teasing over the spot where a mate would mark me, sending shivers of pleasure through me. "Even better than I imagined, and I've been building it up in my head all week."

I threw my leg around his hips, keeping him in place, and realized he was still in his sweatpants. With a hand on his chest, I shoved him to his back, climbing over him.

Cocky as ever, Casey put his hands behind his head, grinning up at me. "The view is even better, too."

I grabbed my chest, closing my fingers around my nipples as Casey's eyes went pure gold, his hands replacing mine in an instant. With a smirk, I slid down his body, fingers sliding inside the waistband of his sweatpants and boxers, tugging them down.

Needy, I wrapped my hand around his cock. Casey sucked in a breath the moment my mouth closed around him, letting go a string of expletives as he brushed my hair out of my face.

"I lied," Casey groaned, "*this* view is the best I've ever seen."

A smile tugged at my lips as I popped him free, kissing and nipping my way around his body.

A deep groan drew my eyes up to his as his hands locked under my arms and pulled me up his body, settling my hips over his.

"It's been way too fucking long, and I need you right now."

Needing no further encouragement, I sank down on him, a moan escaping me as he filled me.

We moved in a perfect rhythm, not wasting even a second trying to find what worked for either of us, letting instinct drive us.

"Couldn't handle a whole week?" I teased.

With a growl, Casey flipped us, my back landing with a thump on the bed as he drove into me again.

"Too many days," he muttered, and I almost thought I heard him add, "Never again," but the sound of the headboard hitting the wall drowned it out.

Grabbing my waist, he tilted my hips, and suddenly I was right on the edge again. I reached for the headboard to anchor myself, and when Casey's eyes locked on me, I lost it.

He hissed at the feeling of me clenching around him, but pulled out before he could join me, smacking my ass.

"Turn."

I'd barely scrambled to my hands and knees before he slammed back inside me. His hands settled on my hips, pulling me back against him, and my mouth fell open as I was lost to feeling.

"So fucking good," Casey panted. Just as he shuddered, his teeth grazed my shoulder, barely holding himself back from biting me.

I reached up, tangling my fingers in his hair as I held his face to my neck, his racing pulse matching mine. I could hardly breathe, but I didn't want this to end. Didn't want to let go.

Casey's arms wrapped around my waist as he fell to his side, tugging me with him. He sighed, then kissed my shoulder. "So fucking good."

Chapter Seven

CASEY

Waking up with Natalie next to me, covered in only my t-shirt, I couldn't resist tracing the soft skin of her hip. Her hair was a mess, her lips swollen in evidence of our night together, and I grinned.

I didn't want whatever we'd just done to be a one-night thing. I wasn't sure how she felt about it, but seeing her in my bed, covered in my scent, I didn't want to let her go.

The house was chilly, the power still out, but I slipped free from the bed, heading to the living room to refill the hopper. Nat was a routine coffee drinker, so I cranked on the gas stove, putting a kettle on to heat up water. We'd have to make coffee the old-fashioned way this morning, but who didn't love a good pour-over. While the water boiled, I grabbed my phone from the coffee table where I'd left it last night, seeing the missed texts from the skulk checking on me.

Sending back a thumbs up emoji to the group chat, I picked up the phone and called my brother.

"Thought I lost you to the storm." Cole's face filled the screen, sitting in the rocking chair in Arrietty's room.

"Nah." I brushed my hand through my messy hair, a slow grin spreading. "All good here."

Cole's dark brows rose, and he tried to hold back a smirk as he typed something on his phone. A minute later, a text from him showed up in the skulk group chat.

COLE

Who had one week?

I flipped him off in the video call. "Hilarious." I wasn't surprised he'd been able to guess what had happened so quickly though. We'd always been able to read each other in an instant. Twin things.

My phone buzzed repeatedly in my hand as the rest of our friends answered the thread, but I refused to look at it.

"Is this a good thing?" Cole asked, lifting Arrietty to his shoulder to burp her. Seeing my brother this domesticated was wild, but knowing I was missing out on it clenched something in my chest.

I shrugged. "How's my daughter?"

"We've been over this. She's not your daughter."

"Well you and I have the same DNA, twin, so she kinda is."

"That's not how that works." Cole rolled his eyes. "I'm also glad you moved out before Arrietty understands your words and you confuse the hell out of her."

Chuckling, I grabbed the teapot, getting the pour-over ready.

"Is that coffee for you?" Cole waggled his brows. "I didn't think you drank coffee."

"I don't."

Cole made his stupid, expectant face, and I heaved a breath.

"Can I ask you something without you making it a whole thing?"

"Probably not."

I finished pouring the water and set the kettle back down. "How did you know? With Skylar?"

He hesitated, studying me. "If you're asking, I think you already know."

"Great. Super helpful."

Grinning, he shrugged. "Can I make it a whole thing now?"

"I'm hanging up on you."

The last thing I heard before I ended the call was my brother bellowing, "SKYLAR! GUESS WHAT —"

"Idiot," I muttered at my blank phone screen, setting it on the counter.

Was he right? Did I already know what I thought I knew?

I raked a hand through my hair, feeling out of sorts, and grabbed the coffee I'd made. In the bedroom, Nat was still asleep. Moving to her side of the bed, I set the mug on the nightstand, and swept her hair off her face. She tended to sleep in, so I didn't want to wake her up, but hopefully the coffee would show I was thinking of her when she woke up and I was gone.

I needed to stretch my legs.

On the back porch, I shifted, my fox eager to check out the snow. It had been too long since I'd had a shifted run. I'd been hesitant to fox out over here on pack lands, but with any luck, the wolves would still be hunkered down from the storm.

I lost track of time as I trotted through the forest, enjoying the brisk air and the cool snow under my paws. Snow fell from the trees overhead, landing on my tawny fur, but everything about the morning was serene.

Here and there I smelled wolves I knew, Darius the Alpha chief among them, but none of the scents were fresh enough to indicate I wasn't alone this morning.

If I listened to my fox, I would mark her with a mating bite. He certainly wanted to claim her. I'd barely held back from biting her last night as it was. But was he just being a horny little shit?

Mine.

Yes, he'd been grumbling that at me all last night as well. Logically, I knew it wouldn't be the same for everyone, but I'd been at the club the night Cole and Skylar met. Their connection was almost instantaneous, practically consummating their mating on the dance floor with a hundred witnesses.

On the other hand, there was Kit and Nimue. They'd been friends for years before he realized what she was to him.

On a good day, shifters were territorial alphaholes, so it

was possible my fox just didn't want anyone *else* to have Nat while we wanted her, and that was why he wanted to claim her.

The thought didn't sit right. I couldn't quite explain it, didn't have any concrete justification behind it, but that just didn't feel like what was going on. Nat and I together had been like no other experience I'd had, and I knew, somehow, that she felt the same way.

My ears swiveled at a crunch in the snow behind me, and I froze, one paw in the air, and whipped my head around.

There, behind me, was a sleek, stormcloud grey wolf with glowing cobalt blue eyes.

Mate.

I stood stock-still as Natalie approached, circling me. Snow dusted her back, giving her a majestic, half-wild appearance.

She came to a stop in front of me, locking eyes for a minute. Before I could register her intention, she stomped the ground right in front of me with both paws, puffing snow up and into my face, then took off in a run.

I smirked, giving her a head start. So she wanted to play, did she? She was about to learn how much faster I was.

Sprinting after her, I trailed her through the woods, letting her stay just enough ahead of me that she thought she had a chance. Then I'd nip at her heels, and take off, making her chase me instead. We zigzagged through the trees until both of us were panting hard, our breath fogging the air, and we slowed to a trot to head back to the house.

Somehow, we'd spent most of the day out in the snow, and the sun was already slanting towards the horizon.

Ambling up the back steps, we shifted back. Nat's face was flushed with the cold and the exertion, her blue eyes brighter from the time as her wolf. Gorgeous.

I tilted my head to the house. "Warm shower?"

She smiled, then yelped as I hauled her over my shoulder, arm around her legs to keep her in place, and jogged to the bathroom.

Chapter Eight

NATALIE

The house was dark by the time we were done showering, steam billowing out into the hall. Fortunately, the water heater was gas, as the electricity still hadn't come back on. I wrapped the towel tight around my chest as I darted for the stairs, headed to my room.

As I put on my leggings and a hoodie, footsteps creaked on the stairs.

"It's freaking freezing up here," Casey said as he came up behind me, wrapping his arms around my waist. He dropped a kiss to my shoulder, his hands slipping under the hem of my hoodie to lay flat on my stomach, as if we hadn't just had sex in the shower minutes ago.

"Considering we're practically self-heating furnaces as shifters, cold isn't as much of an inconvenience as you're making it out to be."

"Shh." Casey nudged the collar of my hoodie aside to kiss my neck, his warm breath skating over my skin. "You're ruining it. It was a good line, and the perfect excuse to insist you come downstairs and snuggle me all night."

I grinned, turning in his hold to put my arms around his neck. I wanted to inhale freshly-showered-Casey deep into my lungs, his body wash only emphasizing his usual woodsy scent. "You could have just asked me to come downstairs."

"Or I could throw you over my shoulder and carry you down. Worked out pretty well last time I did that."

I cocked a brow, barely containing my laugh. "You mean an hour ago?"

"Too soon, I know. I can't have you thinking I'm a total caveman."

Stepping out of his hold, I grabbed his hand. "Come on, needy boy. Let's go make some hot chocolate."

His blue eyes grew two sizes. "Do you have marshmallows?"

"Are you five?"

"Yes. If it means I get marshmallows."

Tugging him behind me, I rolled my eyes, his warm chuckle making something inside me bubble in contended bliss.

"Would you rather live on a giant marshmallow in a hot chocolate lake you could never drink, or only drink hot chocolate without marshmallows the rest of your life?"

"*Only* hot chocolate? Nothing else?"

"Nothing else. Not even water."

"Those both sound like terrible options."

Casey shrugged, passing me on his way to the kitchen, mussing his dark hair. "Life's not fair. You gotta learn to make hard choices. It's almost like you've never played *Would You Rather* before. Terrible options is the whole point."

"I haven't," I answered as I grabbed the cocoa powder and the marshmallows from the pantry.

Casey turned in slow motion towards me, his mouth hanging ajar. "How is that even possible?"

I shot him a *What can you do* look as I started heating milk on the stove. His head tilted in bemused awe, rubbing his jaw.

"A *Would You Rather* virgin. I didn't know there were any of you left." He leaned his hip into the counter next to me, arms crossed as he looked me over. "Consider this your bootcamp."

"What?"

What followed was a rapid-fire string of ridiculous questions, each somehow more insane than the last.

I now knew we'd both rather have a unibrow than no eyebrows at all, would rather slide down rainbows than jump on clouds, and loved the idea of duck-sized elephants.

It was surprising how many we had in common, even if they were completely useless opinions.

"Last question," Casey said as he sat on the couch, our hot chocolates drained and on the coffee table. He pulled me onto his lap, straddling him, and put his hands around my waist. I draped my hands over his shoulders and ran my fingers through the hair at his nape, curious about the suddenly serious set of his face. "Would you rather have a mate connection snap into place instantly, or let one grow over time?"

My hand stilled, heart stuttering over a few beats. All

day, the question had lingered in my mind — was this *it*? Was the instant ease around Casey a mate bond? Was that why I'd acted so out of character by inviting him to live with me about ten seconds after officially meeting him? Had my wolf already known and taken control of my mouth before my brain could catch up and talk her out of it?

"You can't tell me this doesn't feel different to you, too," he went on, like he could sense the thoughts swirling in my mind. And maybe he could, if this was what he thought it was.

"I don't know if there's a right answer to that question," I finally said, carefully watching his reaction. "Is it instant chemistry, or can it build?"

"I don't know either." Casey shrugged, his eyes drifting down, but his fingers tightened on my hips. "I was there when Cole met Skylar, and it was like watching the *Wizard of Oz*, when suddenly the whole world is in color for the first time. He was so positive, and they never looked back."

I slid my hands down his neck, tilting his face back up to mine. "It's not always like that. Look how long Kit and Nimue danced around each other before anything happened. My parents dated for two years before a mate bond settled in, too."

His blue eyes flashed amber, his fox just under the surface as he pulled me more snuggly against his chest. "I don't want to wait a lifetime for my mate when I think she's sitting right here on my lap."

A hesitant smile crept over my face. I leaned forward and kissed him, feeling the heat pass between us despite the snow outside. I'd meant it to be chaste and quick, but neither of us were capable of pulling back, an intrinsic magnetism luring us closer, deepening our kiss.

Chest heaving, I finally broke away, willing my mind to come back to the moment and to form a coherent thought. "I don't know if this is a mate bond yet, but I do know the chemistry between us is like nothing I've ever felt before, and my wolf agrees. So maybe we just keep doing this" — I ground my hips down against him, earning a groan from his throat — "until we figure it out."

At that moment, my phone buzzed, and a second later, Casey's did as well. He fished his out first, frowning at the screen, and I couldn't help but read the notification too since it was right in front of me.

I raised a brow at him. "Did you set up an alert for when my business gets a new review?"

"No," he said, not looking at me as he opened the notification to read the full review. "I set up an alert for when that troll leaves you a new review."

"Hm. Is that cute or stalkery?"

His eyes flashed amber for a split second as his gaze cut to me, then back to his phone. "Stalking comes with the territory. I'm a fox. You said he keeps making new accounts to post negative reviews from so it makes it sound like this is a repeat thing with your clients, so I set up an alert any time a new review is left from his IP address."

"Really, that guy is no big deal, Case." I tried to push his phone hand down, but it didn't budge. "I honestly don't care."

"*I* care."

I blinked at him as something blossomed in my chest.

"So, now what? We just have proof it's all this same guy?"

Casey looked up from his phone with a sly grin. "Need I remind you *I'm a fox?* Now, we cause mayhem."

My brow furrowed. "I'm not sure that's a good idea. He's a human. And this is my business."

He tapped my hip. "Relax. I'll keep it human friendly."

"What the hell does that mean?"

His grin was all teeth. "Don't you want to find out?"

"Nothing illegal?"

Casey tilted his head as he considered that. "If you insist."

I chuckled. "Well, *I'd* insist you do nothing—"

"— which is already off the table —"

"— so I guess the least you can do is not get yourself arrested."

"Plenty of wiggle room there. Watch and learn, Nat. Watch and learn."

With that, he unceremoniously picked me up and plopped me down beside him, already up and striding towards his room and no doubt, his computers.

And damn if a male on a mission to defend my reputation didn't make my heart swell.

Chapter Nine

NATALIE

A fter Casey disappeared into his room to do who knew what for what ended up being the rest of the evening, I packed up the rest of the decor for the New Year's party. Between the two of us crafting every evening, we'd managed to fill a few boxes worth of decor, which hopefully would be enough to give Val and Caedmon the "Enchanted Masquerade" of their dreams.

As much as I was curious what he intended with my troll, no matter how I tried to get him to reveal his plans, he wouldn't budge. And I tried *all* the resources at my disposal over the next few days. Even the annoying *Tell Me, Tell Me Now* song I wrote and played for him on my guitar was to no avail.

"You're trying to annoy it out of me?" he'd snorted. "Really? I have a twin brother. I'm immune to annoyance."

I'd chucked my guitar pick at him.

Christmas week came quickly, and I answered the knock at the door, finding an absurdly large box on the porch.

"Uh, Case?" I called, and he rolled back from his desk to look out his bedroom door. "Is this for you?"

His eyes expanded and he hopped up, chair toppling over, and shoved me away from the door. Sliding on his boots, he grabbed the package, and made his way across the yard to the empty shed I'd never done anything with besides store unused equipment for both the band and my business. "You saw nothing!"

He wrenched open the shed door and disappeared inside, and I crossed my arms against the chill, pulling my sweatshirt sleeves down over my hands. "That was weird."

Casey spent the better part of the afternoon in the shed, and much of the next week as he carried package after package back there. I could hear power tools going whenever I paused my guitar playing, so I knew he was building *something*. Like with the troll, none of my attempts to get him to spill his secrets worked. The male was a vault.

In between whatever he was doing in the shed, we spent our days in almost constant contact, inseparable and insatiable for each other.

I tried to blame it on the snow outside, making the roads dangerous, and the fact all my clients canceled either for weather or for the holidays. But the truth was simpler — we couldn't get enough of each other, whether we were making our way through my eight DVDs cuddled on the couch, making lasagna together in the kitchen, or pursuing more adult activities in the bedroom. Or the shower, or the sofa, or everywhere else in our small home. Some nights if he still had work to do, he even made me come hang out in his room while he finished up just to be near me, so I'd bring in my guitar and we'd coexist in comfortable peace.

I was desperate to talk to someone else who'd found their mate, to compare experiences and see if I could make sense of what was going on with me and Casey. Were we just horny and lonely and had found each other just in time for cuffing season, or was this something more? But my closest female friend was my cousin, and she was single. No help.

Standing at the kitchen window on Christmas Eve, I watched Casey emerge from the shed, a giant grin on his face as he practically hopped across the yard. He threw open the door, the cold air making his cheeks rosy, and instantly, my body reacted to his presence. I'd never been this attracted to someone before, never been this physically needy.

His eyes turned that familiar molten amber, but he shook his head, breathing deep, before opening them back to his usual blue. "Merry Christmas, Nat. Want your present now?"

"Christmas isn't until tomorrow."

"True, but I want to give it to you *now*."

I chuckled, but put my hand in his outstretched palm. After all the secrecy, I was as impatient about this surprise as he was. Sliding my feet into my boots, I followed him across the lawn to the shed, desperately in need of a fresh coat of paint this spring.

With a dramatic flourish, Casey yanked the door open, and I gasped, a hand flying over my mouth. He'd gutted the inside, drywall now covering what had been bare studs, an industrial style chandelier hanging from the center of the room, and LED lights glowing from the baseboards gave the room a distinctly rock'n'roll vibe. It was even heated now. I stepped inside, seeing my guitars hanging on the back wall next to an amp and a recording set-up.

Everything I'd haphazardly stored in here was hidden in a wall of cabinets to my right, and the rest was arranged into a recording studio/lounge space.

"You did *all* of this?" I asked as I turned in a circle, noticing all of the small details he'd included. Framed photos of dogs catching treats in their mouths hung on the wall, combining my two passions in one space.

He scratched the back of his head, an almost sheepish look on his face. "Do you like it?"

"Are you kidding me?" I gaped. "This is amazing. I don't understand how you did all of this in the last week."

"Well, you wouldn't let me cut any more penis-snowflake chains, so I had to find something to do."

I smacked him in the chest, and he gripped my hand, holding it against him.

"I'm serious. This is a lot of work. Where did you even get those photos? They look like my clients."

"They are," Casey nodded. "I had Nimue help. I tracked down your clients and asked if they wanted to be part of your new marketing in exchange for portraits, and Nimue took the pictures. Blaze hung the dry wall while I kept you otherwise occupied at night, and his weird little demon construction company painted everything. I thought about sound-proofing, but there's no one nearby to disturb and I want to be able to hear you practicing from the house. The rest was just furniture assembly really. Well, and the wiring. And I asked Dillon what you'd need for a recording studio to make sure you had everything. I wanted to paint the outside too, but I figured that would be too much of a giveaway and you'd probably want to pick the color yourself. But I did get some options that I think would look good with the house."

I gaped up at him, listing all these things like it was nothing for him to do all this work for me, in addition to continuing to work his full time job as I knew he had been.

Pulling his face down to mine, I pressed my lips to his. His arms wrapped around my waist, fitting me more closely against him.

"I think you might be a little crazy, but this is amazing. I love it." I pulled back enough to press our foreheads together and see his lips quirk into a grin. "But I have a confession."

"What?"

"My gift for you seems totally lame now."

He chuckled, taking my hand to head back to the house. "All I need is you, naked in my bed, and I'm good."

Back at the house, I grabbed his wrapped present from under the tree and handed it to him, curling up next to him on the couch. He shook it, listening for any rattle and trying to work out what the pathetically small box could be.

"Would you just open it? Stop playing with your food."

He scoffed. "Never."

But finally he tore open the wrapping paper, his eyebrows shooting up as he saw the new headphones I'd ordered him.

"I noticed your old ones were a little… duct-taped together."

"These are the ones I kept meaning to order!"

I gave him a playful shoulder punch. "You're not the only one who can be a stalker. I tracked down your brother's number and asked him what kind to get you."

"They're perfect," he said, setting the box on the coffee table.

"I need to find something else now you did all that in the shed," I shook my head. "You went above and beyond."

With a growl, he was on top of me, pressing me into the couch and sinking his weight between my legs. "I'm sure I can think of something you can give me." His teeth grazed along the juncture of my neck and shoulder, sending shivers through my body.

"Oh yeah?"

"Yeah." He pushed up my sweatshirt, laying gentle kisses along my stomach. Then he said the last thing I expected in that moment. "Come with me to Foxing Day?"

He peered up at me, his chin resting on my hip, his eyes wide and surprisingly somber for the words he'd just spoken.

"Sorry?"

"Foxing day."

"You're making shit up again. Like the IP thing all over again."

He nipped my hip. "Am not. Foxing Day is tradition. It's the day after Christmas –"

"-- that's *Boxing* Day –"

"And we all go hang out at Kit's house."

"We all?" I tilted my head. If this was some bros-only Christmas after-party, I didn't want to crash it.

"Kit, Nim, the kids, Cole and Skylar and our daughter, Emerson, Nadir, Akil, Lily and Sophie probably, maybe Nim's mom." He shrugged. "You know. The O.G. skulk and partners. Games, gifts, too much food."

I blinked at him, stunned he'd want to invite me to what sounded like a fairly intimate, if casual, party of his closest friends, when we hadn't known each other very long.

Then my brain circled back to one part.

"Did you just say *our* daughter?"

"Well, since Cole and I have the same DNA, technically speaking..." he trailed off, grinning, and I threw back my head on a laugh. "Please? I want you there this year."

I met his eyes, feeling my own shift to the glowing blue of my wolf to meet the amber of his fox, and nodded. "Then I'll be there."

———

Christmas Day itself dragged on forever. As much as I loved my family and my pack, all I could think about were how many minutes stood between me and seeing Casey again. He had his own family Christmas day to go to, so we'd said a steamy, prolonged goodbye for the day in the shower this morning.

Still, I knew my family could scent him on me by the lingering looks I received, their eyes full of questions. I admitted I was seeing someone, because how could I not, but for some reason felt reluctant to reveal much more. Like if I said out loud I thought he might be my mate, it would break whatever spell Casey and I were under and I'd realize how ridiculous that sounded.

But the more this went on between us, the harder it was to deny. Whether we were mates or not, I was quickly falling for my roommate.

Chapter Ten

NATALIE

"Are you nervous?" Casey shot me a glance and squeezed my hand as we walked up Kit's front steps for Foxing Day.

"A little," I admitted, biting my bottom lip. I didn't know why I was nervous. I'd been on stage in front of thousands of people before, human and supernatural alike, but this was Casey's skulk, his pack. Even if I knew most of them at least in passing from living in the same small town, this was a whole new context. I knew Casey had already talked to Cole about our potential mate-hood, if not the others as well. Would they all be judging me? Assessing if I was mate-worthy, skulk-worthy to join their established family?

"They'll love you," Casey assured me, not bothering to knock before he opened the front door, tugging me inside with him.

Immediately, the scent of Christmas greeted us, cinnamon and spruce and cloves. Someone had been very busy baking, and when Kit popped his head around a doorway, oven mitts on his hands and plaid apron on, it was clear who.

"Close the—" Kit started as a blur of red shot past his feet, gunning for the front door.

Casey's arm shot out, plucking the tiny fox cub from the ground before it could escape outside and holding it by its scruff. I closed the door before another escape attempt could be made, smiling as Casey *tsk*'d at the cub.

"Nice try, Phoenix," he said, gently plopping the cub back on the plush area rug and giving him a nudge. "Off you go."

With a disgruntled harrumph, Phoenix took off like a shot, zooming through the house like his tail was on fire.

Which, I realized a split second later, it was. The very tip of his tail was, indeed, a tiny spark.

Casey saw me watching Phoenix and grinned, sliding his hand to the small of my back to push me further into the house. "They really did make tiny fire-wielding fox Pokémon babies."

Entering the kitchen, we found a world of chaos and laughter. Greetings came from the living room off to the side, faces I recognized waving at us. At the kitchen island, a small girl sat propped in a high chair, "decorating" some cookies, which mostly consisted of her making a mess of sprinkles and frosting.

Kit closed the oven, sliding a tray of gingerbread foxes onto the stove to cool before taking off his oven mitts to greet us. The sleeves of his green sweater were rolled up, revealing his swirling skulk tattoos on his bronze skin, and he pushed thick dark hair out of his amber eyes as he smiled at me.

"Natalie, glad you could join us," he said, wrapping me in a hug before I could register what was happening.

Casey held up a bottle I hadn't noticed he carried. "I brought your wife —"

In a blink, Nimue appeared out of nowhere, snatching the bottle from him and planting a kiss on his cheek. "This is why you're my favorite twin."

From the couch where a board game was underway, Cole shouted an indignant, "Hey!"

"Bring me demon wine and we'll talk, Thing 2," Nimue shot back, unfazed, and moved off to find a corkscrew, long brown hair swishing behind her

"Imagine if someone talked to your children like that," Cole muttered, returning to the game.

"Oh, dear, you've really given this fox quite a large —" Nimue's mother, Morgaine, began, eyeing the decorations Kit and Nimue's daughter was giving to her latest cookie. "—What exactly are you making, Ember?"

"Moose!" the girl pointed enthusiastically at her creation. "Win-moose!"

"Oh, yes I see," Morgaine breathed a laugh of relief. "Yes, usually the antlers go on the head, not between the legs, but it's your interpretation, sweet one. As you were."

Turning her attention to me, she smiled. Where the witch had found a magenta pink light up Christmas palm tree sweater was beyond me, but it suited her. "Natalie, dear, how lovely to see you! How are the decorations for the masquerade coming along?"

"Natalie is a woman of many talents," Casey answered as his hand rested on my lower back, leaning in to kiss my check before moving into the living room to sit next to his brother. He lifted Arrietty from the carrier strapped to Cole's chest, snuggling the tiny baby, and my heart raced. Casey looked up, catching my eye as he kissed his niece's face, then put her up on his shoulder like he was an old pro at this.

I'd never thought much about mating and family before, but suddenly, seeing him here surrounded by his skulk and their children... well, I didn't *not* want this someday.

"Men and babies," Nimue murmured appreciatively as she came to a stop at my side. "Why is this my darn Achilles heel?"

I chuckled, but couldn't disagree with her.

"So, you and Casey, hm?" Morgaine said, holding a cocktail to her lips and raising a white brow above the frame of her oversized teal glasses.

Suddenly, conversation ceased, the board game stopped, and everyone in the room was looking at me, waiting for my answer. Casey smirked, then nudged the table with his foot, upending the board.

They all refocused on the game, arguing over who had been where, Akil calling out, "Phoenix! Get him!" before the tiny fox attacked Casey, running up his leg and over his chest to nip at his ear as Casey pretended to fight him off.

"My son is not your attack dog!" Kit barked at them.

"Attack *fox*," Emerson amended with a smirk.

Nimue rolled her eyes at them and dragged me down the hall away from the party.

"Come help me in the garage," she said, a mischievous look on her face that branded her so very *demon*.

Once in the garage, she whirled on me, all pretense gone.

"So, Kit says that Cole says that Casey thinks you're mates?"

I laughed. "What is this, ninth grade?"

Her black eyes glittered. "Well that wasn't a no."

I shrugged, my heart fluttering as Nimue handed me trays of appetizers from the spare fridge. While I didn't know Nimue well, I'd always liked her. And who else did I have to ask about this? My own family was a mixed bag of supernaturals, and only my parents were mated, but asking them seemed a little awkward.

"I honestly don't know if we are. Is that weird?"

Nimue shut the fridge, turning back to me. "I don't think it's *weird*, per se. I knew I was in love with Kit before I understood I could even be his mate. And I'm sure Casey's expectations of a mate bond are a little skewed after Cole and Skylar's insta-love moment at the club. I've never seen anything like that before though, so I don't think that's the norm either. How do things feel between you two so far?"

"I mean, it's been two weeks, so I don't know. Great? Fun? He's nice." I studied the floor, now feeling dumb for even voicing this. How could I say I'd fallen for someone this fast out loud? If I didn't have a mate bond to blame this on, I needed to get my head checked.

Nimue bumped my hip, then made for the door, a smile

on her face as she looked back over her shoulder. "I, for one, hope you are Casey's mate. We always need new girls in the skulk, and I've always liked you. But even if you're not, come around more."

I nodded, liking Nimue that much more as we made our way back to the kitchen. Right up until she whispered to Kit, "Check the pack bonds. Can you feel Natalie with Casey yet?"

The problem with whispering in a room full of shifters is it's the equivalent of shouting. All conversation in the room stopped, again, everyone turning expectantly to Kit.

There was a reason I'd never tried to be a frontman for our band — I hated being the center of attention, especially with the topic at hand.

As if sensing my unease, Casey crossed the room to me, hauling me into his chest so I could hide my flaming red cheeks. "Don't answer. We'll figure it out on our own, in our own time."

I laced my arms around his waist, soaking in his warmth, ignoring everyone else.

Phoenix chose that moment to go up in flames in his high chair, a delighted shriek coming from beneath the fire as Nimue scooped up her son and pinned him to her chest, her own demon powers putting out the fire as quickly as it started. "Easy, baby. You can't do that."

"Never a dull moment around here, is there?" Morgaine came up to me as Casey rubbed my back and stepped away. Mo held out a cocktail and I took it, though I didn't dare to actually drink it. Her beverages were known to knock immortals out, let alone me.

Before I knew what she was doing, Mo's fingers slipped around my free hand, circling my wrist. It was a weird gesture, but I didn't know her well enough to pull away, so I waited for the moment to pass. She dropped my hand soon after, something unreadable in her eyes, and gave my arm a loving pat. "Just as I thought."

Casey called for me from the couch, and Mo waved her hand to dismiss me. I went to his side, and Casey sat me on his knee, his hand resting on my leg as he leaned toward the game board.

I draped an arm around his shoulders, leaning into his chest as he played, not paying attention to the game at hand. The skulk argued over the rules and teased each other mercilessly, but the love between all of them was undeniable.

"You good?" Casey rubbed a hand across the top of my thigh.

I nodded, feeling at home here in his arms. What more could I ask for?

Chapter Eleven

CASEY

The windows rattled as another storm raged outside Scallywags, giving New Year's Eve a decidedly dark feel. We'd had a lot of snow over the last few weeks, but tonight we were probably headed for another white-out. The lights flickered overhead as they so often did in severe weather. I checked my phone for the forecast, but it didn't look like this was going to get any better as the day went on.

"Why don't we reschedule the party, Caedmon?" Blaze asked, staring at the empty bar, occupied only by those of us who had been here all day setting up. Natalie had gone next door to Dillon's apartment an hour ago, getting ready with Kymari. My suit was hanging in Blaze's office, but I hadn't bothered to put it on yet, thinking this whole thing was about to be called off.

"Because you only get one five-hundredth anniversary, Blaze," Caedmon whined, looking at his husband. "We met on New Year's Eve at a masquerade. All I wanted was a masquerade to celebrate once more."

Val tittered over his husband, kissing his cheek and hugging him tight.

Blaze leaned in to my side. "Did you know this was an anniversary party, or am I just that used to tuning them out?"

I shook my head, staring at the two men. "Why didn't they just say that from the get-go, rather than making this a fundraiser for Winston's love shack?"

"Love is love, my man." Blaze clapped me on the back. "Who are we to stand in the way?"

"So we're not canceling the party, then," Orion muttered from the front door, his annoyance barely contained.

"The show must go on," Val said, nodding firmly.

I finished hanging the paper chains I'd spent the last several weeks making, watching as Morgaine bewitched the ceiling to look like the night sky. Candles hung around the room, suspended midair as they floated above our heads. Suddenly, my paper snowflakes seemed completely unnecessary, but Caedmon gushed over every one, not noticing that I'd cut dicks into as many places as possible. A true ode to the hosts.

"Why did Natalie and I do all this if you could just wave your hand and make it look spectacular?" I asked Morgaine as she walked around the room, the bar magically transforming into a ballroom fit for a fundraiser anniversary masquerade.

Her wrinkled hand came out and patted mine, fingers

looping around my wrist as she squeezed. "It's all magical, dear, even your cock-flakes."

Blaze chose that minute to walk into the bar, cringing. "We've talked about this, Mo. Use your dirty words out of earshot of your children."

"Oh, that's what it is," Val commented, studying the paper chains. "I thought they seemed oddly pleasing to the eye."

I exchanged a glance with Blaze, both of us fighting not to laugh, and Mo winked before we moved apart to continue our different tasks.

It wasn't long before the place was ready and guests started to filter in. We ended up putting a tarp down at the entry way as a de-snowing zone for people to either magic themselves dry or shed their snow-covered coats without traipsing it all over the floor. More people showed up than I was expecting, but maybe Orion had come through with the semi-threatening town messaging system, insisting we all show up. If the roads were too bad to drive home later, Blaze, Nimue, and Nox could run a demon flickering taxi service.

I adjusted the cuffs of the dark suit I'd changed into a little while ago, utterly unable to stop my head whipping around every time the bell jangled over the door, hoping it would be Natalie.

I couldn't lie. When Nimue had asked Kit if he could feel her in our bonds, my heart stopped for a second, waiting to hear what he would say. He'd met my eye, but his expression was unreadable. Could he feel her? Would he even be able to, since she was a wolf? I knew he could feel Nimue, but she was his mate, so maybe it was different.

That didn't stop me from trying to feel along our bonds, seeing if I could find any trace of her. The strongest bonds in my magic were, first, to Kit as my Alpha, and then to Cole, as my blood, with fainter lines to the others in our skulk with varying strength based on how well I knew them.

But so far, no Natalie. I tried not to let it bother me. Whatever we had was going great, with or without a mate bond.

"You look like you need a drink, brother," came Cole's voice from my side as his hand clamped onto my shoulder, giving me a squeeze. He had a simple black mask with red stitching. "Barkeep, two of your finest ales."

Akil popped up behind the counter, maskless, and gave Cole an unamused expression at his words. Apparently, the littlest Sayana had started working here at some point, or maybe he was just working tonight for extra cash.

"Ignore him." Skylar rolled her eyes behind her red mask and elbowed her mate in the ribs, but Akil chuckled as he slid a few drinks over to us. He was a good-natured kid, despite taking all our teasing his whole life.

"So." Cole took a sip of his drink, slipping his arm around Skylar's waist as we leaned back against the counter to observe the room. "Where's Natalie?"

"Still getting ready with Kymari, I think. Where's our daughter?"

"My mom came out for a few days, so they're at home," Skylar replied, completely unfazed by the way I referred to Arrietty. Another reason I liked my brother's mate so much.

She took a sip of her drink, then choked and spluttered out a, "Oh, wow," that had me turning to see what had startled her.

My mouth dropped open as my gaze settled on Natalie entering the bar in front of Dillon and Kymari. She wore an off-the-shoulder cobalt blue dress, fitted from collarbone to her hips, then draping elegantly to the floor. Her gold mask had several cobalt gems decorating it to match the dress, the blue a perfect match to the glowing eyes of her wolf, and my fox immediately rose to attention at the sight of her. Her honey-brown hair was gathered into loose curls that hung down over her shoulder, exposing one side of her neck completely.

My teeth itched, aching to shift to my canines and bite her.

"He's all grown up." Cole pretended to be choked up, and without sparing him a glance, I smacked him in the stomach hard enough for a satisfying *oof* before striding towards my m—

Natalie. My Natalie.

"You're breathtaking."

She blinked up at me, like I'd appeared out of nowhere. Maybe I'd crept up a little too quietly. Fox things. I grinned.

Natalie made no attempt to hide her perusal of me, her fingers trailing down my suit jacket lapel and back up my tie, giving the knot a playful tug I felt straight to my dick.

"You clean up pretty good yourself."

I nodded towards the bar. "Can I get you a drink?"

Nat smiled, threading her arm around mine, and her honeysuckle scent wafted over me as I led her to the bar.

While we waited for our drinks, Darius approached us, and I fought not to straighten up nervously. I knew the wolf Alpha and Police chief from around town, of course, but I had no idea what he would think of Natalie and me being together.

When Natalie brightened at seeing him though, not an ounce of anxiety on her face, I relaxed.

"Darius," she greeted him with a hug, then pulled back and gestured to me. "You know Casey, right?"

I held out my hand, shaking his firmly as he met my eye and nodded with a frown. "Of course. I'd heard you moved in to Natalie's house. On pack land."

Shit, should I have asked him first? "Yes, sir." *Sir?* What the hell was happening to me? I'd never "sir"'d anyone in my goddamn life.

Then Darius broke into a grin, clapping me on the shoulder. "Relax, man. I'm messing with you. If you're good enough for our Natalie, you must be a decent guy. Despite the, uh, disagreements you might have had with the pack in the past."

I cleared my throat. "Thank you?"

Darius turned to Nat, nodding at me. "Bring him for a run sometime."

Her eyes widened. "Are you sure?"

Giving my shoulder another squeeze before dropping his arm, he smiled again. "I'm sure if you are, Natalie."

Grinning, she pressed into me, dipping her head. "Thanks, Darius. I'll bring him soon."

As soon as he left, I raised a brow at her. "A run? Like a pack run?"

She nodded enthusiastically. "It'll be fun."

"Will I get eaten?"

She squinted her eyes. "Probably not."

I took a long sip of my drink as Akil finally slid one to a chuckling Natalie.

"Relax, the pack won't care," she assured me. "No one batted an eye anytime Lily joined us."

I considered that, having forgotten for a minute that Lily used to run with them all the time, back when she was seeing Julian.

"Besides, if anyone gets feisty, we all know you can run faster than any of them," she added, her eyes twinkling with mischief. "Unless you're worried one of them would be faster than you?" She took a sip of her drink innocently, and I narrowed my eyes. I knew a taunt when I heard one.

"You're on, wolf." I clinked my glass to hers.

We made our way around the room as it grew more and more crowded despite the weather. Everyone seemed to be waiting for something, so the details about this secretly being an anniversary party for Val and Caedmon must have leaked at some point. Knowing them, this had been exactly their intention by keeping it a "secret."

No gossip spread faster than secrets in our town.

Just as I pulled Natalie to the make-shift dance floor, the music cut out and the lights flickered, then dimmed.

"You've got to be kidding me," Orion grumbled as he dropped Devanna's hands, striding away as he grabbed his phone from his pocket and stood near the door. Fortunately, between the magicked floating candles and the night sky ceiling, there was still enough light to see around the dim space, setting the mood even more so for the themed masquerade.

Metal clinked on glass to gain everyone's attention, and we turned to see Val and Caedmon standing on a small raised stage on the far side of the room.

"We are happy to announce that our little party has been a success, and we'll begin the construction of Winston's humble abode as soon as possible," Caedmon announced. More than a few glances were exchanged around the room, none of us buying that pretense any longer. He cleared his throat, reaching for Val's hand, drawing him closer. "As some of you may know, tonight is our five hundredth anniversary, and we're honored to spend the evening with you all, our closest friends."

He dabbed a handkerchief at the corner of his eye, and Val took over, nodding to Akil to the side of the stage. Akil bent down out of my sight, fumbling with some equipment, then stepped back, an unsure look on his face as he held up the now useless plug. Mo patted his shoulder and flicked her hand. "I've got it, dear."

Fog billowed around the stage, and the dining room descended into darkness, the candles floating closer to illuminate only Val and Caedmon.

A round of hoots and hollers went up, egging them on.

"Let's hear this story!"

"Finally, the facts!"

"Once upon a time," Val began in a booming voice, waving a hand dramatically, fog swirling around him, "there was a *murderer*."

"*Oooo*," went off around the room, followed by chuckles.

"The culprit? A nasty, evil old vampire who'd decided he didn't care about remaining hidden anymore. He began killing and bleeding his way through the aristocracy of London without a care in the world, leaving behind a trail of grisly corpses, dismembered and drained of blood."

"Is this a love story?" Natalie whispered to me, and a grin tugged at my lips as I shrugged.

"There were two men, one, a servant" — Val gestured at Caedmon, who had draped a towel over his arm like a butler — "and one, a noble's son." Val doffed a top hat he'd popped on from nowhere. "Both of them intent on justice for the evil fiend, though neither knew of the other's plans. With an upcoming ball, the noble's son hatched a plan to trap the evil vampire and end him" — Val brandished a wooden stake — "once and for all!" He lowered his voice, adding, "Little did he know the servant planned to do the same."

The candles flickered for a moment, brightening the dining room just enough for us to see the boxes of popcorn that appeared in all our hands. Blaze stood across the room, the demon grinning at Petra as he fed her a piece of popcorn. No doubt, this was his doing.

"Then what?" Peg Fernsby called from a booth, leaning forward on the table excitedly and munching her popcorn.

"The ballroom was exquisite," Val sighed wistfully. "*Everyone* who was anyone was there, let me tell you. Despite my father's wishes for me to dance with all the ladies — he was trying his best to marry me off — I kept to the edge of the ballroom, watching and waiting. Finally, I thought I spotted the killer. A *very* suspicious looking servant" — he jabbed a thumb Caedmon's way — "who kept hovering around the guests, clearly eavesdropping on them. *Aha!* I thought. Of course, a servant would go almost unnoticed. *That's* how he must be getting away with it!

"It didn't hurt that the servant in question was extraordinarily handsome. Who wouldn't follow that face into darkened alleys, hoping for a moment of his undivided attention?"

"Oh, you." Caedmon blushed.

"So the next time the servant slipped out of the room, I followed him, stake at the ready, tucked into my jacket."

"Was he already a vampire?" I whispered to Nat, who shrugged, her eyes wide as she listened and ate her popcorn.

"I stalked about the manor, intent on finding him and putting him down," Val continued, miming the motions the same way he did every year at the Harvest Fest. "Only, I turned a corner, and he was gone. Vanished. Then I heard a thump from a nearby room" — he placed his hands over his chest, a startled expression selling the story hook, line, and sinker — "so I ran in, just in time to see the servant being attacked!"

"The vampire had followed us from the ballroom, and attacked me first." Caedmon nodded, his face tipped towards his husband and hero. "And it wasn't a male at all, but a female."

Someone in the audience gasped, and Val's eyes lit with excitement. I couldn't help but chuckle at the show.

"One of the very women my father had wanted me to dance with and woo!"

"She sank her fangs into me, quickly draining me of blood —"

"And I came at her with a roar, but then she turned and leapt on *me* instead —"

"Val met my eye over the vampire's shoulder as she drank him, his fingers feebly trying to indicate the stake he'd brought with him," Caedmon chuckled. "And here I was thinking he was happy to see me, with that stake in his pocket. Such a foolish lad, trying to take on that vampire on his own."

"It worked!" Val defended himself. "You managed to get the stake while she was occupied trying to kill me, and staked her yourself."

"Our very first murder," Caedmon murmured lovingly, wrapping a hand around Val's shoulder.

Natalie gaped at me. "Have they had *other* murders?"

"How romantic," Peg Fernsby sighed.

"It turned out Caedmon had lost quite a lot of blood," Val went on. "He used the very last of his strength to kill the vampire, saving my life."

"So then Val saved mine."

Everyone in the room leaned forward almost imperceptibly.

"I turned him."

A racket broke out, half the room shouting, "I knew it!" and the other half groaning, then pulling out their wallets to hand over cash. Apparently there had been more than a handful of bets placed on how their vampiric nature had come about.

"Val's family are all born vampires," Caedmon said. "And while I'd suspected the existence of vampires, I hadn't been able to confirm it until that night, when one was at my throat. Even as I lay there in a pool of my own blood, I knew that, if I lived, I'd never be able to go back to my regular, human life. Not after knowing the truth." Caedmon found Petra's eyes in the audience, exchanging a knowing nod with her. "When Val asked, it was a no-brainer."

"He'd also been obsessed with me for months," Val added, beaming.

"Love at first bite?" Blaze chuckled.

"What about your father? The ladies?" Peg called out.

"Well, as scandalous as it was for me to fall in love with *a servant*," Val grimaced, "my father knew better than to try to get in the way of true love."

Caedmon patted Val's arm. "He sent us away the next week, both to get me out of the way while I was *adjusting*, and to avoid the scandal of his son running away with the help."

Val nodded. "Banished from society."

"Never to return."

"No regrets." Val turned his face up to Caedmon's, pressing their lips together. "Not a one."

"You knew he was the one? Just like that?" someone called from the crowd, but I couldn't see who.

"I took off his mask, and that was it." Val shrugged.

"I'd never wanted anyone like I wanted him in that moment, and for every moment thereafter."

Peg clapped emphatically, tears shimmering on her cheeks beneath her mask, and pretty soon others joined her, applauding the strange vigilante-murder-love story.

As the vampires left the stage to mingle, I met Natalie's perplexed expression, no doubt wearing one of my own.

"I have far more questions than answers," she laughed.

"I think that's always the way with those two," I agreed, and we tossed our popcorn boxes in the trash before heading for another drink.

Chapter Twelve

Midnight approached swiftly, Akil using a Bluetooth speaker he had connected to his phone, which someone had magicked to play loud enough for the whole bar. The lack of power didn't slow this crowd down a bit as the bar became a self-serve free-for-all the later into the night it got. Both the skulk and the pack were here, and everyone seemed to be paying closer attention to Casey and I than seemed normal, but I smiled and shook hands with everyone who sought us out.

All the while, Val's words kept swirling in my mind, how he just *knew* more or less the minute he saw Caedmon that night.

Wasn't that what had happened with Casey and me? I invited him to live with me as soon as I met him. That wasn't normal.

Dancing with him among our friends, candlelight glowing around us, I couldn't remember the last time I'd felt this at ease, had this much fun. And it wasn't only the party — it was like this all the time when we were together.

Was this what love, what *mates* were supposed to be? Just — easy?

I peered up at him, his eyes darkening and flashing amber, and wondered if he was this mixed up about me as I was about him.

Opening my mouth, I was about to ask him just that when he leaned down, mouth at my ear. "Take a walk with me."

My heart fluttered at his tone, sultry and the perfect amount of demanding, and I nodded. I slid my hand into his as he tugged me towards the door and grabbed our coats, holding mine for me as I put it on.

Together, we strolled outside, snow falling steadily as he led me towards the gazebo. Winston stood nearby, ornaments hanging from his antlers the way they always seemed to be this time of year, and I wondered what tree he'd left bare of decorations. Somewhere, there was a weird Charlie Brown tree, mauled by the friendliest moose on the East Coast.

We stepped into the gazebo and I looked up at Casey, loving the way the white snow contrasted against his dark hair. But maybe I loved everything about him.

My phone dinged in my pocket, breaking my focus when his did the same.

Casey pulled his out, smiling at the screen.

"What is it?" I asked, trying to peer at his phone.

He held it out, showing a street view of a house I recognized.

"Is that the troll's house?" I tugged his phone free, staring down at the grainy image.

"Sure is," Casey said as he moved behind me, wrapping his hands around my waist and leaning over my shoulder. "I programmed it so every time he leaves a nasty review for not only you, but other companies too, a giant troll doll is delivered to his house. This is the street-view camera from the intersection across from his house."

As he said it, a delivery van drove down the street, stopping in front of the house and blocking the camera. I waited with bated breath as the van delivered something, then left.

In the middle of the bare lawn stood a four-foot tall Troll doll, pink hair standing on end and a jewel shining in its belly. I laughed, turning to look at Casey over my shoulder. "Well, that's kind of funny."

"Keep watching." He pointed at his phone, a smirk forming. "The best is yet to come."

My ex-client answered the door, saw the giant Troll doll there, and immediately carried it to the trash bin on the side of his house. By the time he turned the corner, walking back to the door, the Troll was back, but now, there were two of them, half the size as before.

I frowned, looking back at Casey. "I thought we said no magic."

"It's harmless, I promise."

Again, my disgruntled client carried the two new Troll dolls to the trash, placing it in the bin with the giant one, and again, he returned to the front door to find four more

Trolls. Each time he threw them away, they doubled until there were dozens of miniature Trolls decorating his lawn.

"Who did this?" he shouted, hands on his hips as he looked up and down the dark street, but no one was there. Finally, he gave up and went inside, slamming the door.

Casey took the phone from my hands, and I chuckled, shaking my head. "I should have known you'd resort to some sort of prank."

"Well, I am a fox." Casey grinned. "We do love to be sneaky."

I turned in his hold, draping my hands around his neck. "Thank you," I said with a slight shake of my head. "This was the strangest way to have my honor defended, and yet it feels so very you. I love it."

"Good," Casey beamed, his hands tightening around my waist. "I want to kiss you at midnight."

I laughed, expecting that signature smirk to be on his face, but quickly stopped at his serious expression. His gaze honed in on mine, no trace of humor anywhere.

"Good," I mirrored his words with a smile, and finally, his lips twitched.

"*Ten, nine*" — the countdown began inside the bar, the sound muffled from out here but still audible with our shifter ears, the whole bar joining in on the chant.

Casey's hands cupped my jaw, his thumb tracing over my cheek, his eyes searching mine as he removed my mask, a look of pure adoration written in every line of his face.

"*Two, one —*"

Cheers and poppers drowned everything else out, but

all my focus was on Casey anyway. He met my lips, a hand dropping from my face to my hip, tugging me closer. His tongue traced the seam of my lips, and I opened for him, deepening our kiss as fireworks shot through my body, every inch we were in contact feeling like it was in contact with a live wire.

Holy fuck.

I jerked back. The words hadn't been my own thoughts. Or had they?

Casey frowned. "Is something wrong?"

"Did you —" I broke off, searching through my magic, then looking around the square. Had that been someone from the pack? Wolves could communicate with their Alphas telepathically, and sometimes other wolves we were very close to, but we were the only ones outside right now.

I love you, I thought in my head, aiming it in Casey's direction to test what I thought had just happened.

His eyes widened, flashing between amber and blue.

"What was that? How did you" — he tilted his head, eyes narrowing and dropping to my lips — "your mouth didn't move."

My breath caught. "You heard me?"

"I — I guess so?"

Then, faintly, I heard, *You love me, huh?* and I grinned.

His lips quirked too. "Did I do it? Foxes don't speak like that in our heads so I'm not sure how it works."

"You did it," I assured him, though I knew it would take him some practice to be able to communicate as clearly and easily as I could.

Does this mean what I think it means? came next.

I brushed a stray snowflake from his cheek. "I don't know how it could be anything else."

Suddenly, I yelped in surprise as my feet left the gazebo floor, my butt landing on the railing as Casey stepped into me.

"Well, thank fuck," he breathed, his nose already at my neck. "Because I love you too, *mate*." He growled as my dress constricted our movements, not letting him press as close to me as I knew he wanted.

"I need to get you home," he muttered, nipping along my jaw.

I tilted my head back, enjoying him tasting me. "Roads don't look great, Case."

He pulled back, a deviant glint in his eyes.

"What?" I asked hesitantly.

"I know how we can get home safely, and fast."

Catching on, I pretended to consider it. "It's pretty far."

He shook his head. "Not that far. It'll be faster than driving." His voice lowered to a rumble that had me shivering in anticipation. "I need you, mate. *Now*."

Grinning, I pushed him back so I could hop off the railing. "It's going to cause a scandal when someone finds our clothes out here tomorrow."

Casey snorted, already shedding his coat. "Let it."

In seconds, we dropped our clothes and shifted.

I met his amber eyes, tilting my head. *Race you.*

I took off like a shot, and Casey quickly caught up, staying by my side as we raced back to our house, leaving our pawprints in the snow behind us.

If this is what being your mate feels like, Casey's voice rang in my head, *I'll gladly chase you for the rest of my days.*

THE END

Want more Deadlights Cove?

There's more to come in the Deadlights Cove universe!

Join our newsletter at aimeevancebooks.com to be the first to know!

Smoke Show

Deja Brew

A Very Merry Christmoose (Novella)

Wing and a Miss

Pier Pressure

Karma is a Witch

Foxing Day (Novella)

Coming Soon

Timber Creek Series

Acknowledgments

For each and every one of you who reached out to tell us you weren't ready for the Cove to end... Well, neither were we.

A huge thank you to those of you who have poured love on *Deadlights Cove* in reviews and posts online. We are thrilled to see that you love it as much as we do!

Amy, Brit, Elle, and Lex: Thanks for helping us keep this secret!

XO,
Aimee and B.

About the Author - B. Perkins

B. has been making up stories about magic since she learned how to write words on paper. When not immersed in fictional worlds, she enjoys spending time in nature. She has several degrees in various things, and if all they're good for is to provide background in creating fantasy worlds and systems, then maybe they were worth it.

About the Author - Aimee Vance

Fueled by peach tea and chaos, Aimee Vance believes that life doesn't end for romantic heroines in their early twenties and that everything would be better if magic was real, both of which are prominent themes in the stories she tells.

Outside of writing happily-ever-after endings for hot-mess heroines, she spends her days with her husband, two young daughters, and a rambunctious labrador retriever in Texas.

———

Also by Aimee Vance

Fates Illuminated
Fates Promised
Fates Defied — May 2024

 instagram.com/aimeevancebooks

Made in the USA
Columbia, SC
14 December 2024

48213000R00067